W9-BZA-348

For Anne McNeil
K. G.

To my family
M. McQ.

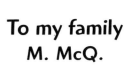

Text copyright © 2003 by Kes Gray

Illustrations copyright © 2003 by Mary McQuillan

First published in Great Britain in 2003 by Hodder
Children's Books, a division of Hodder Headline Limited,
338 Euston Road, London NW1 3BH

First published in the United States by Holiday House, Inc.
in 2004

The right of Kes Gray to be identified as the author and
Mary McQuillan as the illustrator of this Work has been
asserted by them in accordance with the Copyright,
Designs and Patents Act 1988.

All Rights Reserved

Printed in Hong Kong

www.holidayhouse.com

First American Edition

1 3 5 7 9 10 8 6 4 2

Library of Congress Cataloging-in-Publication Data

Gray, Kes

Cluck o'clock / written by Kes Gray; illustrated by Mary
McQuillan.—1st American ed.

p. cm.

Summary: A group of chickens has a full day on the farm,
from eating breakfast early in the morning to avoiding a
fox late at night.

ISBN 0-8234-1809-X (hardcover)

[1. Chickens—Fiction. 2. Farm life—Fiction. 3. Domestic
animals—Fiction. 4. Stories in rhyme.] I. McQuillan, Mary,
ill. II. Title.

PZ8.3.G7433C1 2004

[E]—dc21   2003050845

CLUCK

Written by Kes Gray

Holiday House / New York

O'CLOCK

Illustrated by Mary McQuillan

It's 4 o'cluck in the morning.
Another day is dawning....

Colin the rooster
puffs out his chest.
Ready to do
what he doodle-doos best.

5 o'cluck. The farmer appears.
With toast in his hand and soap round his ears.

5:05. He unlocks the door.
Rattles his bucket. Throws corn on the floor.

We gobble our breakfast in ten seconds flat.
Jessie's the fastest (that's why she's so fat).

6 until 8. We sit on our nests. We lay white eggs or brown eggs.
(Marge does requests.)

Just after 8. We leave the hen coop.
And stroll round the farmyard all in one group.

From 9 until 10. We go our own ways.
The dust bath is Freda's,
the hopscotch
is Faye's.

11 o'cluck. We meet by the plow.
Squabble and squawk about what to do now.

If the tractor's been busy, we might hunt for worms.
Big ones, little ones, anything that squirms.

12 o'cluck. We sit in the trees.
Ambush some caterpillars, lacewings, and bees.

12:25. We practice our clucks.
Tell a few jokes and dive-bomb the ducks.

1:02. We walk down the lane.

Jane is the blackbird who lives in the hedge.

Jane is an expert on earwigs and slugs.

One for the exercise. Two to see Jane.

She has a family of four and a husband named Reg.

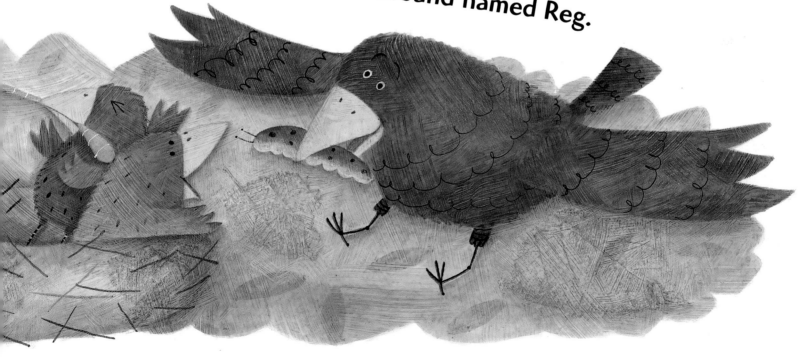

She knows where to find the tastiest bugs.

2 o'cluck. We play hide-and-seek.
Valerie should learn to tuck in her beak.

3 o'cluck. We lie on our backs.

We find shapes in the clouds and then we make tracks.

4 o'cluck. We're back in the yard.
Wally the Collie is standing on guard.

Call him a guard dog? He's totally useless.
Woofless, furless, and totally toothless.

4:15. We go
to the stable.

To visit the horses,
Molly and Mabel.

4:30 till 5. We perch in the rafters.
Watch them eat grain and hope for some afters.

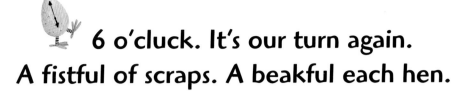 6 o'cluck. It's our turn again.
A fistful of scraps. A beakful each hen.

 7 o'cluck. We form a long line.
And wait for the farmer to give us the sign.

When he jangles the keys from inside his pocket,
   points to the henhouse, and bangs on his bucket...

We race to the coop in fifty-eighth gear.
   Faye and Marge bring up the rear.

Last to the perch is a big rotten egg!
   (Anne isn't playing. She's got a bad leg.)

The farmer locks up and goes in to eat.
Pork chops and gravy will be tonight's treat.

7:30. We're ready for bed. No one is tired, so we chatter instead.

 8 o'cluck. The sun starts to fade.

The henhouse grows darker. Light turns to shade.

9 o'cluck. The farmer shows up.
With hot milky coffee in his favorite blue cup.

He rattles our door and checks all the locks.
We sit on our perch and wait for the fox.

The fox is named Olga. She lives in the wood.
She eats chickens for supper. She'd eat us if she could.

Brenda starts fidgeting at 20 to 10.
Any time now will be fox time again.

At 10:57 we all hear a sound.

Something is sniffing
and snuffling around.

The noises are coming from the farmhouse back door.

Trash bags are spilling out onto the floor.

Tin cans are clanking.

Pork bones are cracking.

Sharp teeth are crunching.

Olga is snacking.

The farmer is sleeping.
He doesn't hear her.
But we can hear sounds creeping nearer and nearer.

Feet or inches, it's too dark to tell.
But Olga is close.
We can tell by the smell.

Colin stays calm
and jumps to the floor.
Just to the left of the
crack in the door.

Through the hole in the wood, he wiggles a feather.
(Very kindly donated by Heather.)

He wiggles it, jiggles it, and now you'll see why.

When he takes it away, it's replaced by an eye.

It's greedy, it's beady, it's nasty and vulgar.
It's stary and scary.
It's definitely Olga.

Before Olga can blink, Colin scoops up some dirt.
And gives her an eyeful, right where it hurts.

Olga runs off with a flea in each ear.
That will teach her to come sniffing round here.

It's 12 o'cluck midnight. Everyone's yawning.
Time for some sleep. Only four hours till morning!

THE HEND